CUPCAKE CATAPULT!

Adapted by Frank Berrios

Based on the teleplay "Rusty's Flingbot"
by Jack Ferraiolo

Illustrated by Luke Flowers

A GOLDEN BOOK • NEW YORK

T#: 521468
ISBN 978-1-5247-6540-8
randomhousekids.com
Printed in the United States of America
10 9 8 7 6 5 4 3 2 1

ANNUAL
CUPCAKE CELEBRATION

"Here it is!" announced Rusty at the town park. "For this year's annual Cupcake Day celebration, I present the Cupcake-o-Matic 5000!"

"Perfect!" said Chef Betty. "This is gonna be the best day ever!"

"Hmm. You know, instead of handing out cupcakes the boring way, what if I built something really cool?" suggested Rusty. "Like a cupcake-throwing Flingbot!"

"I think I'd prefer a robot waiter that hands people cupcakes gently," said Chef Betty.

"We can make that!" replied Ruby.

"Thanks!" Chef Betty gave Rusty and Ruby a big plate of cupcakes. "Take these to test your robot."

"This may be the best job ever," said Ruby. She and Rusty raced away to get started.

Using parts from the Recycling Yard, Rusty and Ruby built an amazing robot.

"Introducing Flingbot, the best cupcake-flinging robot on the planet!" exclaimed Rusty.

"But Chef Betty doesn't want a cupcake-flinging robot," Ruby reminded him.

"Only because she doesn't know how awesome it will be!" Rusty flipped a switch and powered up the robot. "Let's see if it works. Flingbot, find cupcake."

Flingbot grabbed a cupcake and tossed it into the air. "Cupcake, fling!" said the robot.

Flingbot worked—a little too well! The robot was also throwing things that weren't cupcakes.

"Maybe Flingbot doesn't know what a cupcake is," said Rusty.

Just then, Liam arrived wearing his catcher's mitt.

"Hi, guys!" he said. "Why'd you make a robot that throws stuff and calls everything a cupcake? I think that's my new favorite game!"

Suddenly, everything went quiet.
"Where did Flingbot go?" asked Ruby.
"Oh, no—it escaped!" cried Rusty. "If it gets anywhere near the park, Chef Betty's Cupcake Day will be ruined!"

"We have to shut Flingbot down," said Rusty.

"Here's the plan," said Ruby. "You guys cause a distraction. Bytes and I will sneak up behind Flingbot and hit the Off switch."

"Great idea!" replied Rusty.

But the plan fell apart when Bytes spotted the colorful squeaky toys Flingbot was tossing. Bytes couldn't control himself—he just had to chase them!

"Flingbot is heading right for the park!" said Rusty. "We have to warn Chef Betty!"

"Rusty! Ruby!" said Chef Betty. "The Cupcake-o-Matic 5000 is amazing! Is the robot waiter almost ready?"

"Well, about that . . . ," Rusty began.

"Cupcake, fling!" commanded Flingbot as trash cans and tires flew through the air.

"Rusty, I told you I didn't want a Flingbot," said Chef Betty.

"I'm sorry," replied Rusty. "I thought you'd change your mind if you saw how cool it was."

"But it doesn't even know what a cupcake is," Chef Betty protested.

Rusty had to find a way to make things right. He quickly grabbed a cupcake.

"Flingbot," he said, "this is a cupcake!" Then he turned to Ruby. "Quick, scan it!"

"Scanning and sending to Flingbot!" replied Ruby.

Flingbot blinked as it studied the cupcake. “Cupcake . . . fling?” it said.

“It worked!” cried Chef Betty.

Suddenly, Flingbot began snatching half-eaten cupcakes from people and flinging them!

"My Cupcake Day is being ruined! By cupcakes!" said Chef Betty.

"We can fix this," said Rusty. "We just need something to catch all the cupcakes!"

"Let's combine it!" said Ruby.

"And design it!" added Rusty.

Rusty and Ruby raced back to the Recycling Yard.

"We'll start with a wheeled base that can move in all directions," said Rusty.

"Then we'll add four robot arms with giant catcher's mitts," continued Ruby.

"Put it all together and we've got our plan!" finished Rusty.

Rusty and his team went to work. Liam rolled the tires in as Jack and Crush helped Rusty drill them into place. Ruby adjusted the engine with help from Whirly. Before long, they were done.

"Modified. Customized. Rustified!" said Rusty proudly.

Back at the park, Rusty revealed his latest machine. “Say hello to the Catchator 6000!” he said.

Meanwhile, Flingbot continued its work. “Cupcake, fling!” said the robot.

Rusty's new machine jumped into action. "Cupcake, catch!" it cried.

Using its mitts, the Catchator 6000 caught every cupcake Flingbot flung. Everyone cheered!

The flinging and catching continued until finally, the Cupcake-o-Matic 5000 stopped making cupcakes.

"Now there's nothing left for Flingbot to fling!" Rusty said with a smile.

Then Flingbot saw that the Cupcake-o-Matic 5000 was shaped like a cupcake.

"Cupcake, fling!" shouted Flingbot. It tossed the machine into the air!

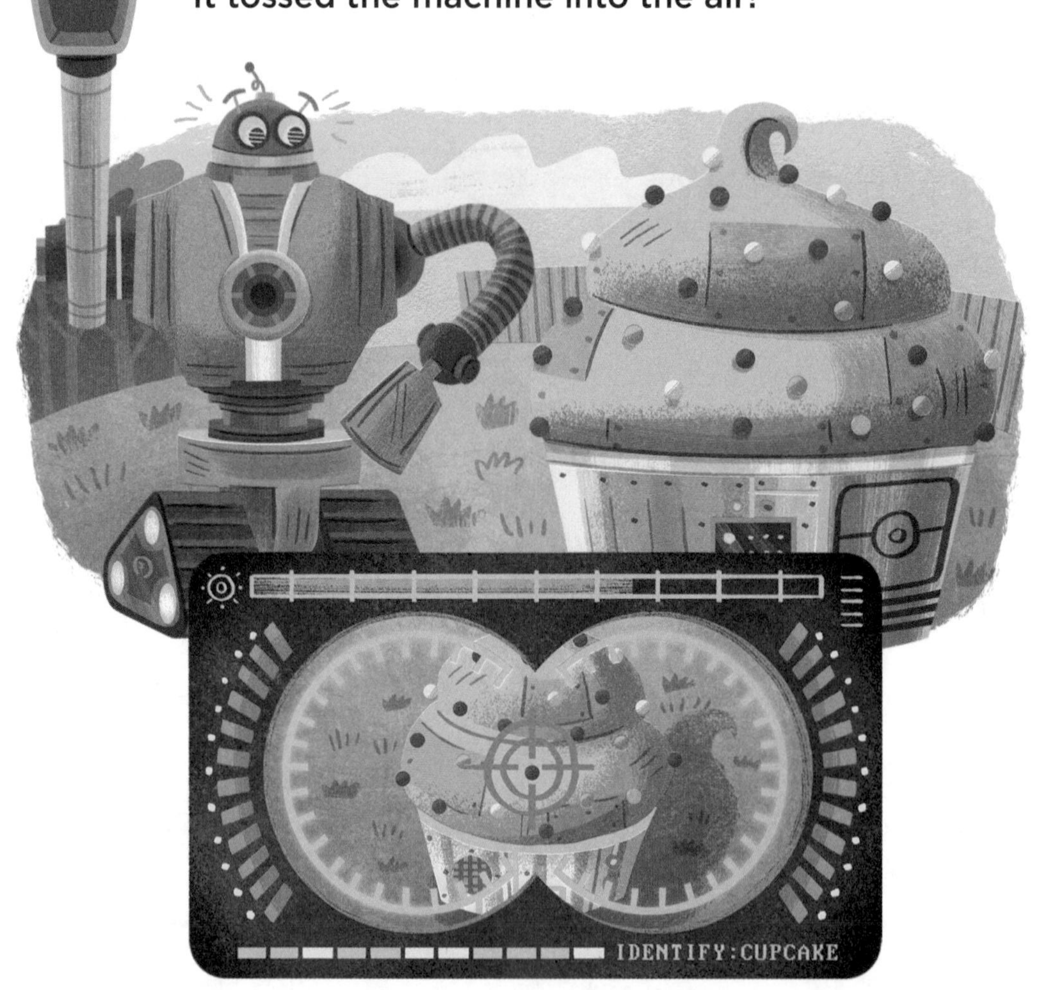

The cupcake maker flew through the sky, but the Catchator 6000 was ready. "Cupcake, catch!" it said.

"Way to go!" said Chef Betty. "Now to make more cupcakes for Cupcake Day!"

Chef Betty added more ingredients to the Cupcake-o-Matic 5000.

Each time the Cupcake-o-Matic 5000 finished a cupcake, Flingbot flung it—and the Catchator 6000 caught it! Everyone worked together to distribute cupcakes.

"Flingbot and the Catchator 6000—the perfect team!" said Ruby.

"It looks like everything worked out after all," added Rusty. Just then, the Cupcake-o-Matic 5000 began to rumble and shake.

"That doesn't sound good," noted Ruby.

"Let's have a look!" said Rusty.

Rusty grabbed his tools and opened the cupcake maker.

"I think I found the problem," he chuckled.

Inside he saw Bytes, happily munching away on cupcakes. It was the sweetest and silliest Cupcake Day ever!